Andy Griffiths lives in a 91-storey treehouse with his friend Terry and together they make funny books, just like the one you're holding in your hands right now. Andy writes the words and Terry draws the pictures. If you'd like to know more, read this book (or visit www.andygriffiths.com.au).

Terry Denton lives in a 91-storey treehouse with his friend Andy and together they make funny books, just like the one you're holding in your hands right now. Terry draws the pictures and Andy writes the words. If you'd like to know more, read this book (or visit www.terrydenton.com).

THAT'S A LOT OF BOOKS.

ANDY GRIFFITHS

The 91-STOREY TREEHOUSE

ILLUSTRATED BY
TERRY DENTON

PAN
Pan Macmillan Australia

First published 2017 in Pan by Pan Macmillan Australia Pty Ltd
1 Market Street, Sydney, New South Wales, Australia, 2000

Reprinted 2017 (twice), 2019, 2020 (twice)

Cataloguing-in-Publication entry is available
from the National Library of Australia
http://catalogue.nla.gov.au

Typeset in 14/18 Minion Pro by Seymour Designs
Printed by IVE

MIX
Paper from
responsible sources
FSC
www.fsc.org
FSC® C018183

The paper in this book is FSC® certified.
FSC® promotes environmentally responsible,
socially beneficial and economically viable
management of the world's forests.

CONTENTS

CHAPTER 1

THE 91-STOREY TREEHOUSE

Hi, my name is Andy.

This is my friend Terry.

We live in a tree.

Well, when I say 'tree', I mean treehouse.
And when I say 'treehouse', I don't just mean
any old treehouse—I mean a 91-*storey* treehouse!
(It used to be a 78-storey treehouse, but we've
added another 13 storeys.)

So what are you waiting for?
Come on up!

It's got a tent with a fortune teller called Madam Know-it-all,

MADAM KNOW-IT-ALL
FORTUNE TELLER

Will I really get a Pony for my birthday?

a submarine sandwich shop that serves sandwiches the size of *actual* submarines,

the world's most powerful whirlpool,

a mashed-potato-and-gravy train,

a spin-and-win prize wheel,

a trophy room,

a human pinball machine,

an air-traffic control tower,

a 91-storey house of cards,

a giant spider web (with a giant spider!),

a desert island,

a garbage dump (with a mysterious old wardrobe on top),

and a big red button (which we're not sure whether to push or not because we can't remember what it does).

As well as being our home, the treehouse is also where we make books together. I write the words and Terry draws the pictures.

As you can see, we've been doing this for quite a while now.

Sure, it's easy to get distracted when you live in a
91-storey treehouse …

but, somehow, we always get our book written in the end.

CHAPTER 2

Madam Know-it-all

new
pants

If you're like most of our readers, you're probably
wondering what that big red button is for.

'Yeah, I've been wondering about that too,' says Terry. 'What *does* it do, Andy? I can't remember.'

'I don't know,' I say. 'I can't remember either.'

'Then let's push it and find out!' says Terry.

'No!' I say. 'For all we know it might be one of those buttons that blows up the whole world!'

'But then again,' says Terry, 'it *might* be one of those buttons that makes a rainbow come out of your nose.'

'Well, yes, maybe,' I say, 'but do you really think it's worth the risk of blowing up the whole world just to see if a rainbow comes out of your nose?'

'Um,' says Terry, 'let me think about that for a moment … um …

um …

um …

um …

um …

'Yes?' says Terry.

'NO!' I say. 'That's the WRONG answer! Whatever you do, DO NOT push that button.'

'But—'

'No!'

'But I—'

'No!'

'But I really, really, really want to know what it does!' says Terry. 'Please let me push the button, please, please, please, pleeeeeeeeeease!'

'No,' I say. 'I've got a *better* idea. We'll go and ask Madam Know-it-all what will happen if we push the button. She'll know.'

'Who's Madam Know-it-all?' says Terry.

'You know!' I say. 'The fortune teller.'

'Of course!' says Terry. 'I knew that … at least I *thought* I did. What did you say her name was again?'

'Don't worry about it,' I say. 'Just follow me.'

We begin the long climb up and then down to Madam Know-it-all's level.

We finally reach Madam Know-it-all's tent and go inside. It's dark and kind of spooky. Madam Know-it-all is sitting at a small round table gazing into her large crystal ball.

'Greetings,' she says, without looking up. 'I've been expecting you.'

'You have?' says Terry.

'Of course,' says Madam Know-it-all. 'I knew you were coming. And I know why you're here. I know all there is to know—past, present and future!'

'If you already know why we're here,' I say, 'then can you tell us the answer to our question?'

'Of course I can,' she says. 'I am Madam Know-it-all. I can tell you the answer to *every* question. I know all there is to know—past, present and—'

'We know!' I say.

'I know you know,' says Madam Know-it-all.

'We know you know we know,' I say, 'so can you just tell us?'

'Yes,' says Madam Know-it-all, 'but not until you *ask* me your question.'

'But you already *know* what our question is,' I say.

'I know,' she says, 'but that's just how this thing works. You ask a question, I tell you the answer in a cryptic rhyme.'

'Okay,' I say. 'What we want to know is: what will happen if we push the big red button?'

Madam Know-it-all peers into her crystal ball and says:

It's very large
And very red—
All who see it
Are filled with dread!

Madam Know-it-all jerks her head back and gasps.

'What is it?' I say. 'What did you see?'

'I saw a big explosion,' she says, 'and then …
DOOM … more *DOOM* … and then even more
DOOM … and then … *nothing.*'

'Just as I thought,' I say. 'Thanks, Madam Know-it-all—we'll see you soon.'

'Sooner than you think,' she replies, as Terry and I step out of the tent into the daylight.

'Well,' I say. 'Now we know for sure. Pushing the big red button will definitely blow up the whole world.'

'I guess so,' says Terry. 'So does that mean we *shouldn't* push it?'

'YES!' I say. 'I mean NO! We absolutely should *not* push that button!'

'But why would we have made such a dangerous button in the first place?' says Terry.

'I don't know,' I say. 'I can't remember.'

'Me neither,' says Terry. 'Anyway, now that we've answered the readers' question, does that mean it's the end of the book?'

'I guess so,' I say.

'But we're only up to page 39,' says Terry. 'It seems a bit short.'

'Maybe we can see if the readers have any other questions they'd like answered,' I say.

'Good idea,' says Terry. 'I'll ask them.'

'Hey, readers! Do you have any other questions you would like answered?'

DOES TERRY HAVE BLOND HAIR?

WHY IS ANDY SO LAZY?

IS MR BIG NOSE REALLY YOUR PUBLISHER?

WHY ARE YOU IN THE BOOK?

DOES MR BIG NOSE REALLY HAVE A BIG NOSE?

ARE TERRY AND ANDY LONG-LOST BROTHERS?

WHAT WILL THE NEXT TREEHOUSE BOOK BE ABOUT?

CAN JILL REALLY TALK TO ANIMALS?

WHY DID YOU MAKE THE BOOKS?

WHY DID TERRY HAVE *ALL* THE ICE-CREAM FLAVOURS?

I LIKE BIPLANES.

WHY DOESN'T JILL LIVE ON A FARM?

WHEN DID YOU START WRITING YOUR AWESOME BOOKS?

WHY DOES TERRY HAVE INFLATING UNDERWEAR?

WHY IS TERRY THE FUNNIEST?

WHEN WILL THE NEXT TREEHOUSE BOOK BE OUT?

CAN YOU MAKE A BOOK CALLED *SPICY JOKES*?

WHY CAN'T JILL HAVE MORE ANIMALS?

WHY DID TERRY FEED HIS UNDERPANTS TO THE SHARKS?

WHY DO YOU HAVE SO MANY PENGUINS?

CAN YOU WRITE A BOOK ABOUT A WITCH CHICKEN?

'I couldn't understand them,' says Terry. 'They were all talking at the same time!'

'They weren't *talking*,' I say. 'They were *shouting*! I don't know *what* they want to know.'

'Hmmm,' says Terry, 'I suppose if *I* were the reader what I would *most* want to know is what's going to happen in *this* book.'

'Me too,' I say.

'If only there were a way of finding out,' says Terry.

'There is,' I say. 'We can ask Madam Know-it-all.'

We go back inside the tent.

'I knew you'd be back,' says Madam Know-it-all. 'You have another question, don't you?'

'Yes, we do!' says Terry. 'Can you tell us the answer?'

'Of course I can,' she says. 'I am Madam Know-it-all. I know … well, I know you already know how much I know, but before I can tell you what you want to know, you must ask me the question.'

'Can you tell us what's going to happen in this book?' I say.

Madam Know-it-all gazes into her crystal ball.

Where once was two
There shall soon be a few.
You'll have an important job to do:
A very busy man is counting on you.
If you let him down, this day you will rue.

I look at Terry.

Terry looks at me.

'I don't get it,' says Terry.

'Me neither,' I say.

'But it's perfectly clear!' says Madam Know-it-all.

'Can you just tell us?' I say.

Madam Know-it-all sighs. 'I can't just come out and tell you,' she says. 'That's not the fortune-telling way. But I can give you a hint—it rhymes with "spaby-zitting".'

'Um … is it … *fraby-hitting*?' says Terry.

'No,' says Madam Know-it-all.

'Um … is it … *shaby-knitting*?' I say.

'No, of course not,' says Madam Know-it-all. 'There's no such thing as shaby-knitting!'

'What about … *babysitting*?' says Terry.
'Correct!' says Madam Know-it-all.

'*Babysitting*?!' I say. 'But we don't have any babies.'

'That's right,' says Terry. 'How are we going to be babysitters if we don't have any babies?'

'You don't have any *yet*,' says Madam Know-it-all, 'but you soon will. Now go and answer the video phone. You have a caller.'

'No we don't,' I say. 'The phone isn't even ringing.'

RING! RING!

RING! RING!

RING! RING!

'Wow,' says Terry. 'You really *do* know everything.'
'I know,' says Madam Know-it-all.

CHAPTER 3

Little Big Noses

We answer the video phone. It's Mr Big Nose, our publisher.

'What took you so long?' he barks. 'I'm a busy man, you know!'

'I know,' I say. 'Sorry. Are you calling about the book?'

'No,' he says. 'I'm actually calling about some babysitting.'

Terry looks at me. I look at Terry. Madam Know-it-all was right!

'I need you to look after my grandchildren,' says
Mr Big Nose. 'They are staying with Mrs Big Nose
and me, but we have tickets to the opera tonight—
Il Bignosio d' Explodio.'

'Is that the story about the guy whose nose gets
longer every time he tells a lie?' says Terry. 'I *love*
that one!'

Idiot!

'No,' says Mr Big Nose, 'that's *Pinocchio*—just a silly children's story. I'm talking about opera— *serious* opera. *Il Bignosio d' Explodio* speaks of matters far above your heads. Art, truth, beauty, exploding noses … in fact, it starts with the most explosive operatic aria of all time! Here, I'll sing it for you.'

'Oh, bravo, bravo!'
says Terry. 'That
was il magnifico
de stupendio!'

'Thank you,'
says Mr Big
Nose, taking
a big bow.

'Um, about the babysitting, Mr Big Nose,' I say.
'I'm not sure that's such a good idea. I mean, Terry
and I are not really qualified.'

'Don't be ridiculous,' says Mr Big Nose. 'You've
both worked in a monkey house, haven't you?
You're probably *over* qualified if anything.'

WHEN TERRY AND I WORKED IN
THE MONKEY HOUSE.

'Yeah,' says Terry. 'Come on, Andy, it will be fun. Besides … what could possibly go wrong?'

'Hmmm …' I say. 'Let's ask the readers.'

'Okay,' says Terry. 'Hey, readers, can you see any reasons why our treehouse wouldn't be suitable for Mr Big Nose's grandchildren?'

'What did they say?' says Terry.

'No idea,' I say. 'They were all shouting at the same time again.'

'They said it would be fine,' says Mr Big Nose. 'And, more importantly, so do I. Here are the twins, Albert and Alice …

and here's the baby—CATCH!'

'Got it!' says Terry, holding the baby in his arms.

'Just as well!' says Mr Big Nose. 'And you'd better take really good care of it—and the twins—because Mrs Big Nose is very fond of her grandchildren. I want them back in my office, safe and sound, by lunchtime tomorrow, along with your new book … OR ELSE!'

'Bye-bye, Pop-pop!' say Alice and Albert.

'Goo-goo ga-ga,' says the baby.

The screen goes blank.

Albert looks around, his eyes wide. 'I've always wanted to visit your treehouse!' he says. 'I've read *every* book.'

'Me too!' says Alice. 'I've always wanted to fight the Trunkinator—I'm going to do it right now!'

'And I'm going to go into the Maze of Doom,' says Albert.

'Me too,' says Alice. 'And for lunch let's have a swim in the chocolate waterfall!'

'I'm not sure we'll have time to do all that,' I say.
'Terry and I have a book to write. You heard what
your grandpa said.'

'We know you've got a book to write,' says Alice,
'but you can keep working while we play. We're
old enough to look after ourselves now. I just
turned six.'

'Me too,' says Albert. 'And we'll be careful. We
promise.'

'Goo-goo ga-ga,' says the baby.

I turn to Terry. 'What do you think?' I say.

'Well,' says Terry, 'they *are* six years old and they *have* promised to be careful.'

'Yeah,' I say. 'And we *do* have a book to write. So I suppose it's okay.'

'Yay!' says Albert, grabbing the baby from Terry.

'This is going to be the best day *ever*!' says Alice as they run off.

'Great,' I say, 'now that the kids are occupied, we can write our book. I don't know what I was so worried about. Babysitting is *easy*!'

'Yeah,' says Terry, 'it's easier than writing a book. Speaking of which, what are we going to write about? Should we ask the readers?'

'Nah,' I say, 'they're a bit shouty.' No offence, readers. (But you are!)

'Here comes Jill,' says Terry. 'We can ask her.'

'Ask me what?' says Jill.

'Any ideas for what we should write about in our next book?'

'Well,' she says, 'what's happened so far today?'

'Nothing much, really,' I say. 'We went to see
Madam Know-it-all to find out what our big
red button does. Then Mr Big Nose rang up and
sang us a song about a man with an exploding
nose. And then he said we had to babysit his
grandchildren.'

'Really?' says Jill. 'He wants *you* to babysit?'
   'Yeah, he and Mrs Big Nose had to go to the
opera,' says Terry.
   'When are the children coming?' says Jill.
   'They're here already,' I say. 'They went off to play.'

'By themselves?' says Jill.

'No, they were all together,' says Terry.

'How many are there?' says Jill.

'Three,' I say. 'Alice and Albert and the baby.'

'Baby?' says Jill. 'Shouldn't you be looking after them?'

'We can't watch them *every* minute of the day,' I say. 'We've got to finish our book and Mr Big Nose will be angry if we don't get it done.'

'I think he'll be even angrier if anything happens to his grandchildren,' says Jill.

'But they promised to be careful,' says Terry.

'It doesn't matter *how* careful they are,' says Jill. 'They could still have an accident. What if they fall out of the tree?'

'That would be bad,' I say.

'Or, even worse,' Jill continues, 'what if they fall into the shark tank?'

'That would be *really* bad,' says Terry, looking worried, 'because the sharks haven't had breakfast yet.'

'But the twins said they were old enough to look after themselves,' I say. 'They just turned six.'

'Six?!' says Jill. 'That is *way* too young to be looking after themselves *and* a baby. We need to find them and make sure they're safe. Let's go!'

We hurry to the chocolate waterfall. We can't see the kids, but it's pretty obvious they were here. There are little chocolate footprints everywhere.

We follow the trail of footprints to what used to be the 91-storey house of cards. But there's no house … and no kids.

We keep looking. We find a baby's bootee on the chainsaw-juggling level. (Fortunately it's empty.)

We go to the ice-cream parlour, but all we find is a very upset Edward Scooperhands.

'They ate it all,' he says, waving his empty scoops in the air. 'Even the invisible ice-cream.'

'Did you see where they went?' says Jill.

'That way,' he says, scooping towards the Trunkinator's level.

We rush to the Trunkinator's boxing ring.

But there are no kids … just the Trunkinator lying flat on his back.

'Wow!' says Terry. 'They must have knocked out the Trunkinator!'

'Poor Trunky,' says Jill. 'But where are the children *now*?'

'I don't know,' I say. 'I think we should ask Madam Know-it-all. She will know.'

We climb the ladder up to her tent as fast as we can.

Madam Know-it-all is hunched over her crystal ball.

'I knew you were coming,' she says. 'What is your question?'

'Do you know where Mr Big Nose's grandchildren are?' says Terry.

'Of course I know,' she says. 'I know all and see all.'

'So where are they?' I say.

Madam Know-it-all stares into her crystal ball.

Round and round
And round it goes,
Where it ends,
Nobody knows (except for me, of course,
because I know everything)!

We all look at each other and shrug.

'Can you give us a clue like you did last time, please?' says Terry. 'We're in kind of a hurry.'

'I know,' sighs Madam Know-it-all. 'All right. Here's your clue: "girl school".'

'They've gone to a girls' school?' says Terry. 'But Albert's a boy and the baby is too young to be at school!'

'No, you fool,' says Madam Know-it-all. 'Where they are rhymes with "girl school".'

'Um … *smirl schmool*?' I say.

'No,' says Madam Know-it-all. 'There's no such thing.'

'Um … is it … *whirlpool*?'
says Jill.

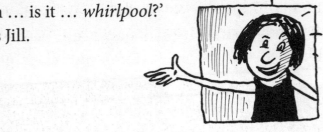

'Yes!' says Madam
Know-it-all. 'I knew
you would get it.'

'Do you mean *our* whirlpool?' says Terry.

'Yes!' says Madam
Know-it-all.

'But our whirlpool is the most powerful whirlpool in the whole world!' I say. 'It's *totally* unsuitable for children.'

'I know!' says Madam Know-it-all.

'Uh-oh,' I say.

'Come on,' says Jill. 'There's no time to lose. We've got to get there before they fall in!'

'Too late for that,' says Madam Know-it-all. 'They already have.'

CHAPTER 4

Whirling and Sinking

We arrive at the whirlpool and discover that
Madam Know-it-all was right again! Mr Big Nose's
grandchildren are whirling around and around and
around, getting closer and closer to the centre with
each whirl.

'Oh my goodness!' says Jill.
'Those children are in
terrible danger! How
do you stop this thing?'

'You can't,' says Terry. 'It's the world's most
powerful whirlpool. *Nothing* can stop it.'

'Look at us!' calls Alice. 'We're in the whirlpool!' 'I can see that,' I say. 'But it's time to get out now.'

'Why?' says Albert. 'The ride isn't finished yet.'
'It's not a *ride*,' I say. 'It's actually a really dangerous whirlpool.'

'We've got to get them out before they get sucked into the middle,' says Jill.

'We'll have to pull them out,' I say.

We get as close to the edge of the whirlpool as we dare and lean out to grab them.

'You can't catch us!' calls Alice as they whirl past, laughing and squealing.

'We'll see about that!' I say. 'Terry, hold on to me so I can lean out further.'

'Okay,' says Terry. He picks me up by my legs and holds me out over the whirlpool.

I grab wildly at the children but I still can't reach them.

'Missed me!' says Alice.

'Missed me too!' says Albert.

'I need to get closer, Terry!' I say.

'Jill!' says Terry. 'Can you hold on to me so I can lean out a little bit further?'

'Sure,' she says. 'I've got you.'

I'm *really* close now. This time when they come around I grab Alice with one hand and Albert—who is holding the baby—with the other.

'Got you!' I yell. 'Terry! Pull me back in!'

'Jill!' says Terry. 'He's got them! Pull me back in.'

'I'm trying,' says Jill, 'but I'm slipping!'

'Me too!' says Terry.

'Uh-oh,' I say.

Now we're *all* in the whirlpool ...

whirling ...

whirling ...

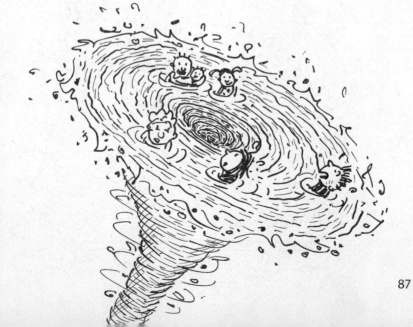

whirling ...

whirling ...

whirling ...

whirling

… until we stop whirling—
get sucked down—and start
sinking!

**SINK
-O-
METER™**

1000 LEAGUES

2000 LEAGUES

3000 LEAGUES

4000 LEAGUES

5000 LEAGUES

6000 LEAGUES

7000 LEAGUES

8000 LEAGUES

9000 LEAGUES

10000 LEAGUES

11000 LEAGUES

12000 LEAGUES

13000 LEAGUES

14000 LEAGUES

15000 LEAGUES

16000 LEAGUES

17000 LEAGUES

18000 LEAGUES

19000 LEAGUES

20000 LEAGUES

Sinking ...

SINK
-O-
METER™

1000 LEAGUES
2000 LEAGUES
3000 LEAGUES
4000 LEAGUES
5000 LEAGUES
6000 LEAGUES
7000 LEAGUES
8000 LEAGUES
9000 LEAGUES
10000 LEAGUES
11000 LEAGUES
12000 LEAGUES
13000 LEAGUES
14000 LEAGUES
15000 LEAGUES
16000 LEAGUES
17000 LEAGUES
18000 LEAGUES
19000 LEAGUES
20000 LEAGUES

sinking ...

SINK
-O-
METER™

1000 LEAGUES
2000 LEAGUES
3000 LEAGUES
4000 LEAGUES
5000 LEAGUES
6000 LEAGUES
7000 LEAGUES
8000 LEAGUES
9000 LEAGUES
10000 LEAGUES
11000 LEAGUES
12000 LEAGUES
13000 LEAGUES
14000 LEAGUES
15000 LEAGUES
16000 LEAGUES
17000 LEAGUES
18000 LEAGUES
19000 LEAGUES
20000 LEAGUES

KLONK!

sinking ...

SINK
-O-
METER™

1000 LEAGUES
2000 LEAGUES
3000 LEAGUES
4000 LEAGUES
5000 LEAGUES
6000 LEAGUES
7000 LEAGUES
8000 LEAGUES
9000 LEAGUES
10000 LEAGUES
11000 LEAGUES
12000 LEAGUES
13000 LEAGUES
14000 LEAGUES
15000 LEAGUES
16000 LEAGUES
17000 LEAGUES
18000 LEAGUES
19000 LEAGUES
20000 LEAGUES

sinking ...

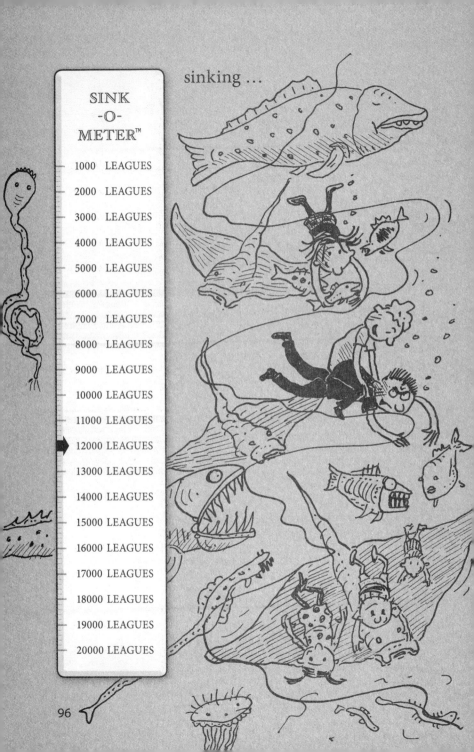

SINK
-O-
METER™

1000 LEAGUES
2000 LEAGUES
3000 LEAGUES
4000 LEAGUES
5000 LEAGUES
6000 LEAGUES
7000 LEAGUES
8000 LEAGUES
9000 LEAGUES
10000 LEAGUES
11000 LEAGUES
12000 LEAGUES
13000 LEAGUES
14000 LEAGUES
15000 LEAGUES
16000 LEAGUES
17000 LEAGUES
18000 LEAGUES
19000 LEAGUES
20000 LEAGUES

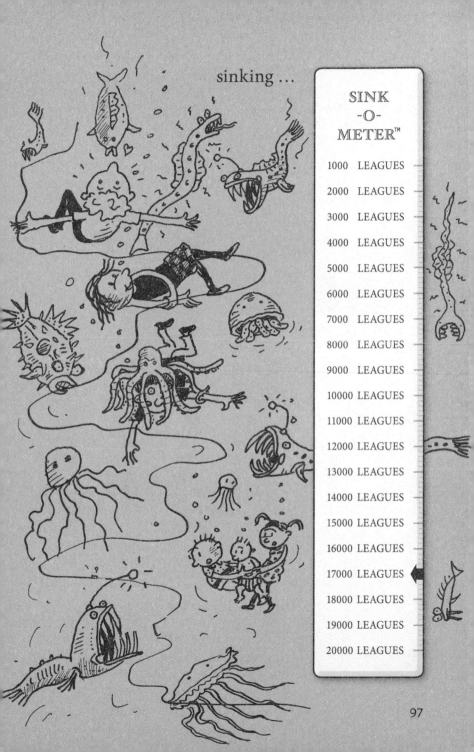

sinking ...

SINK
-O-
METER™

1000 LEAGUES
2000 LEAGUES
3000 LEAGUES
4000 LEAGUES
5000 LEAGUES
6000 LEAGUES
7000 LEAGUES
8000 LEAGUES
9000 LEAGUES
10000 LEAGUES
11000 LEAGUES
12000 LEAGUES
13000 LEAGUES
14000 LEAGUES
15000 LEAGUES
16000 LEAGUES
17000 LEAGUES
18000 LEAGUES
19000 LEAGUES
20000 LEAGUES

… until we hit something soft and sandy and we can't sink any more.

CHAPTER 5

20,000 Leagues Under the Sea

I've got to say it's actually quite nice down here, especially if you like things beginning with the letter 's'. There are seahorses, starfish, stingrays, sand, shipwrecks and a sign saying *20,000 Leagues Under the Sea*. I could be wrong, but unless I'm very much mistaken—and I don't think I am—it looks as if we are …

TWENTY THOUSAND LEAGUES UNDER THE SEA!!!

Like I said, it's quite nice down here. The only problem is that I don't think I can hold my breath for much longer.

I'm not worried, though, because I've got a plan.
Well, when I say 'plan', I mean sandwich. And
when I say 'sandwich', I mean submarine.

Yes, you read that right. I've got a submarine
sandwich from our submarine sandwich shop.
And what you probably don't realise about
these sandwiches is that they not only *look* like
submarines, they *work* like submarines too!
Check it out!

THE SUBMARINE AND SANDWICH
FEATURES OF A SUBMARINE SANDWICH

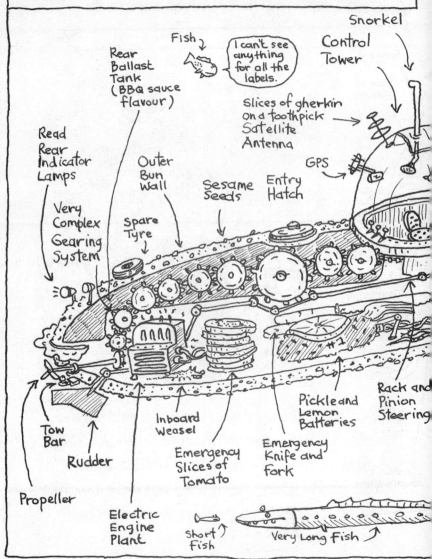

Fish

Snorkel

Control Tower

Rear Ballast Tank (BBQ sauce flavour)

I can't see anything for all the labels.

Slices of gherkin on a toothpick Satellite Antenna

Read Rear Indicator Lamps

Outer Bun Wall

Sesame Seeds

Entry Hatch

GPS

Very Complex Gearing System

Spare Tyre

Inboard Weasel

Pickle and Lemon Batteries

Rack and Pinion Steering

Tow Bar

Rudder

Emergency Slices of Tomato

Emergency Knife and Fork

Propeller

Electric Engine Plant

Short Fish

Very Long Fish

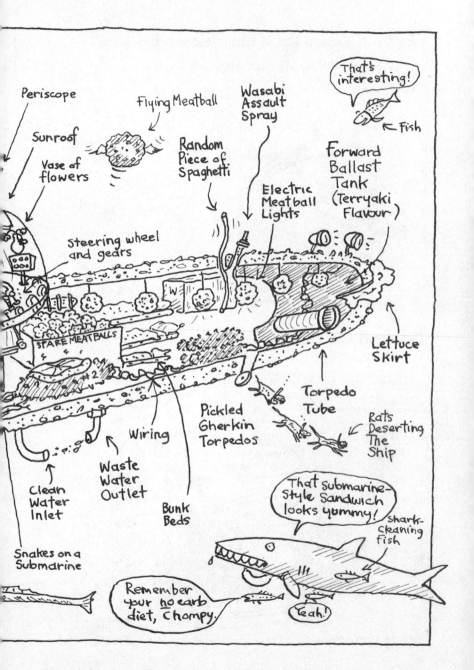

We climb aboard the submarine sandwich and
I make my way to the control deck.

The others join me ...

and I set a course for the surface, twenty thousand leagues above.

'Thanks, Andy,' says Terry. 'Your submarine-sized submarine sandwich saved our lives!'

'It sure did,' says Jill. 'Where did you get it from?'

'From our submarine-sized submarine sandwich shop, of course!' I explain. 'The sandwiches are so big it takes me a couple of weeks to eat them. So I keep them in my pocket and just pull them out whenever I'm hungry. Or whenever I find myself deep underwater.'

'I'm kind of disgusted and kind of glad at the same time,' says Jill.

'I'm glad too,' says Albert. 'I've always wanted to ride in a submarine.'

'And I've always wanted to ride in a sandwich,' says Alice.

'Goo-goo ga-ga,' says the baby.

'This reminds me of that song,' says Terry. 'You know, the one about a sandwich submarine!'

'Do you mean *Rock Around the Sandwich Submarine*?' I say.

'No,' says Terry.

'*Twinkle, Twinkle, Little Sandwich Submarine*?' I say.

'No, that's not it either,' says Terry.

'What about *We All Live in a Sandwich Submarine*?' says Jill. 'That always tops any list of top ten songs about sandwich submarines.'

Top Ten Sandwich Submarine Songs OF ALL Time

1. WE ALL LIVE IN A SANDWICH SUBMARINE
2. TWINKLE TWINKLE LITTLE SANDWICH SUBMARINE
3. DON'T YOU WISH YOUR SANDWICH SUBMARINE WAS HOT LIKE ME?
4. WE WISH YOU A MERRY SANDWICH SUBMARINE
5. ROW ROW ROW YOUR SANDWICH SUBMARINE
6. SANDWICH SUBMARINE ODDITY
7. WHAT A WONDERFUL SANDWICH SUBMARINE
8. LIGHT MY SANDWICH SUBMARINE
9. STAIRWAY TO SANDWICH SUBMARINE
10. ROCK AROUND THE SANDWICH SUBMARINE

'Yes! That's the one!' says Terry. 'How does it go again?'

'Like this!' says Jill, and she starts singing:
'We all live in a sandwich submarine,
a sandwich submarine,
a sandwich submarine ...'

The rest of us join in:
'We all live in a sandwich submarine,
a sandwich submarine,
a sandwich submarine ...'

RISE
-O-
METER™

1000 LEAGUES
2000 LEAGUES
3000 LEAGUES
4000 LEAGUES
5000 LEAGUES
6000 LEAGUES
7000 LEAGUES
8000 LEAGUES
9000 LEAGUES
10000 LEAGUES
11000 LEAGUES
12000 LEAGUES
13000 LEAGUES
14000 LEAGUES
15000 LEAGUES
16000 LEAGUES
17000 LEAGUES
18000 LEAGUES
19000 LEAGUES
20000 LEAGUES

THE DAY WE SAILED BENEATH THE SEA IN A SANDWICH SUBMARINE SINGING A SONG ABOUT LIVING IN A SANDWICH SUBMARINE

We all live in a sandwich submarine, a sandwich submarine, a Sandwich Submarine...

Stop!

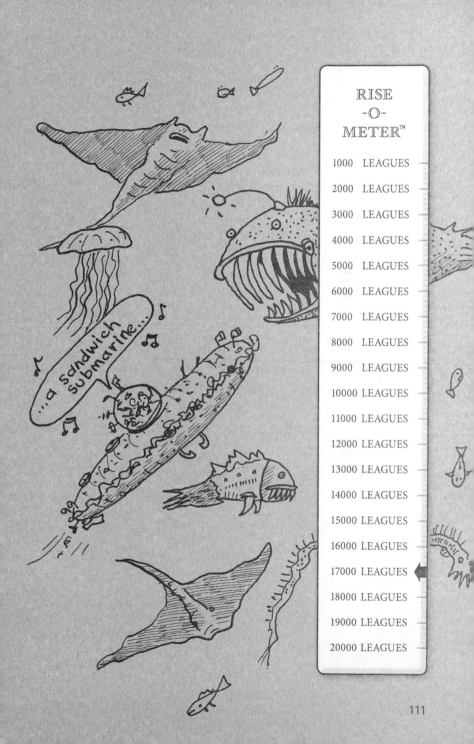

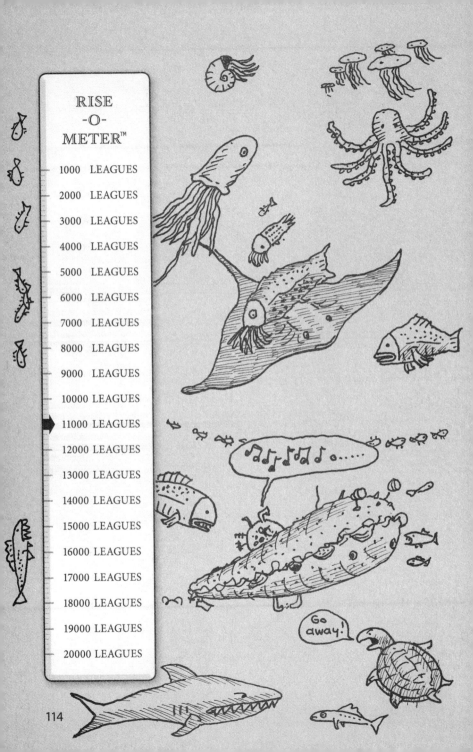

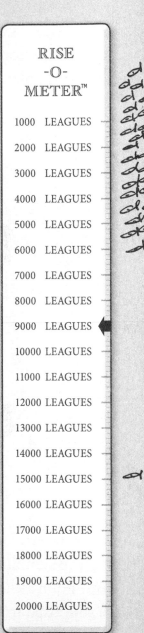

RISE
-O-
METER™

1000 LEAGUES

2000 LEAGUES

3000 LEAGUES

4000 LEAGUES

5000 LEAGUES

6000 LEAGUES

7000 LEAGUES

8000 LEAGUES

9000 LEAGUES ◀

10000 LEAGUES

11000 LEAGUES

12000 LEAGUES

13000 LEAGUES

14000 LEAGUES

15000 LEAGUES

16000 LEAGUES

17000 LEAGUES

18000 LEAGUES

19000 LEAGUES

20000 LEAGUES

'Hey, Andy,' says Terry. 'This is a really fun ride and I don't want to complain, but it's getting really soggy in here! My feet are sinking into the floor.'

meatball

'So are mine,' says Jill.

'The submarine must have sprung a leak,' I say. 'But I don't know how. Submarine sandwich bread is supposed to be 100 percent waterproof.'

'I think I've found the problem,' says Jill, pointing to the deck below. 'The children are eating the submarine!'

'Hey, stop that!' I say.

'But we're *hungry*,' says Alice.

'And it tastes really good,' says Albert.

'I know,' I say, 'but it's also a submarine, and you don't eat a submarine that you're travelling in! *Everybody* knows that!'

'I don't think everybody *would* know that,' says Jill. 'It's an easy mistake to make. We should probably all put on emergency life jackets. Where are they kept?'

'I don't think there are any,' I say.

'What about emergency life boats?' says Jill. 'Does it have any of those?'

'No,' I say. 'I don't think so.'

'Does it have emergency *anything*?' says Jill.

'It's got emergency pickles,' says Terry, holding up a jar.

'What's the use of that?' says Jill. 'Nobody likes pickles. They're the bits you take *out* of your sandwich.'

'What about your emergency automatic self-inflating underpants, Terry?' says Albert. 'Are you wearing them?'

'As a matter of fact, I am,' says Terry.

'Then how come they didn't inflate when you fell in the whirlpool?' I say.

'Because I haven't got them turned on,' says Terry. 'They kept inflating when it wasn't an emergency, and it was a bit embarrassing, so I turned them off.'

SOME OF THE (MANY) TIMES TERRY'S SELF-INFLATING UNDERPANTS INFLATED IN INAPPROPRIATE SITUATIONS

'Can you still activate them?' I say.

'Yes,' says Terry. 'I can operate them manually.'

'Well, what are we waiting for?' I say. 'Everybody hang on to Terry. We'll be on the surface in no time.'

We all grab hold of Terry.

'Everybody ready?' he says.

We all nod.

'All right then,' he says. 'Here we go—3, 2, 1, blast off!'

whoosh!

It's a wild ride, but within seconds we are all floating around on the surface of the sea using Terry's emergency self-inflating underpants as a life raft.

'Yay!' says Alice. 'That was fun!'
  'Let's do it again!' says Albert.
  'No way!' I say. 'We've got to start paddling.'
  'But there's nowhere to paddle to,' says Alice.

'Yes there is,' says Jill. 'Look—over there! A desert island!'

'Goody!' says Albert. 'I *love* desert islands!'

'Me too!' says Terry.

'Goo-goo ga-ga,' says the baby.

CHAPTER 6

Marooned!

We paddle until we reach the island. I jump out into the shallow water and pull the others safely to shore.

'Thanks, Terry,' I say. 'You saved our lives!'

'Don't thank me,' says Terry. 'Thank my underpants.'

'Thanks, Terry's underpants,' I say.

'You're welcome,' says Terry in a high-pitched voice, which I think is supposed to be his underpants.

'What are we going to do now?' says Alice.

'Be marooned,' I say. '*That's* what!'

'How do you do that?' says Albert.

'Easy!' I say. 'You sit around on a desert island with no food, no water, no map and no way of ever getting back to the treehouse.'

'That sounds kind of boring,' says Albert. 'Why don't we get rescued by that ship instead?'

'What ship?' I say.

'That one!' says Albert, pointing to the horizon.

Albert is right. There *is* a ship. A *big* ship.

We all jump up and down and yell and wave our arms like a bunch of wacky waving arm-flailing inflatable tube men at a wacky waving arm-flailing inflatable tube men festival.

'It's not stopping!' says Terry.

'Maybe they can't see us,' says Jill. 'We need to start a fire and make some smoke signals!'

We collect a bunch of driftwood and use a packet of driftmatches to start a driftfire.

I rip one of the biggest leaves off a palm tree and hold it over the fire to smother the flames. Then I pull the leaf away and a big puff of smoke puffs up into the sky. But the ship doesn't stop.

'It's not working,' says Jill. 'They probably just think we're having a barbecue. Let me try making a message!'

I give Jill the leaf and she makes three small puffs of smoke that spell out 'SOS'.

'Let me have a turn,' says Terry, reaching for the leaf.

He waves the leaf over the fire and the sky fills with puffy smoke pictures.

'Terry,' I say, 'how exactly are these pictures going to make the ship come and rescue us?'

'I don't know,' he says, shrugging. 'I just like drawing smoke pictures! You've got to admit they're pretty good.'

'Give me that!' I say, snatching the leaf from him. There's no time to lose. I start fanning out a new message that will leave no doubt about what we want.

It's a pretty clear message, but by the time I've finished there is so much smoke that none of us can see anything.

.....DESERT ISLAND AND WE TRIED TO
....SIGNAL A PASSING SHIP FOR HELP
.....THAT IT FILLED THE WHOLE ISLAND

137

By the time the smoke has cleared, the ship is nowhere to be seen.

'Well, that's just great,' I say. 'You think they would have seen all that smoke—or at the very least *smelled* it.'

'Hey,' says Terry, 'look at this old teapot I just found in the sand.'

'That's not a teapot,' says Jill. 'I think it's one of those mysterious magical lamps that you rub and a genie comes out and grants you three wishes.'

'Cool!' says Terry. 'I'm going to try it.'

He rubs at the lamp and smoke starts billowing out of the spout.

'Oh, no, not more smoke!' says Alice.

'Relax,' I say. 'This is *good* smoke. This is magic *genie* smoke!'

Sure enough, the smoke gets thicker and thicker and then it forms into a ...

GENIE!

'Thank you for releasing me from my prison,' says the genie. 'As a reward, I grant you three wishes.'

'Fabulous!' I say. 'Let's all wish to get off the island!'

'No!' says Albert. 'I want a lollipop. I *wish* I had a lollipop!'

'Your wish is my command,' says the genie.

'No, stop!' I say, but it's too late.

'One lollipop!' says the genie, handing Albert a large lollipop.

'Hey,' says Alice. 'How come Albert got a lollipop and I didn't? I WISH—'

'Don't do it!' I say. 'Don't wish for any more lollipops!'

'—FOR A LOLLIPOP, TOO!' says Alice.

'Your wish is my command,' says the genie. It produces an enormous rainbow-swirl lollipop and gives it to Alice.

'OKAY, THAT'S IT!' I yell. 'NOBODY WISH FOR ANY MORE LOLLIPOPS!!!'

'But that's not fair!' says Terry. 'They got lollipops! I wish *I* had a lollipop, too!'

The genie shrugs. 'Your wish is my *final* command,' it says, placing a lollipop the size of a dinner plate in Terry's hand. 'So long, suckers!'

'WAIT!' I yell. 'Could we please have one more wish?'

'No way,' says the genie. 'I'm all out of wishes and I'm definitely out of here.'

'I WISH you wouldn't go,' I say.

But it's no use—the genie disappears.

'You crazy lollipop-lickers,' I say. 'You wasted all our wishes on lollipops and we're still stuck on the island!'

'Look on the bright side, Andy,' says Terry. 'We might be stuck on an island but at least we've all got lollipops.'

'*I* haven't got a lollipop,' I say.

'Me neither,' says Jill.

'Never mind,' says Terry, holding his lollipop out towards us, 'you can have a turn of mine.'

'Hey, is that another genie lamp?' says Albert, pointing to something in the water.

'No,' I say, as it floats closer. 'That's just a bottle.'

'That's so sad,' sighs Jill. 'Here we are in the middle of nowhere and yet we still can't get away from litter.'

'Hang on,' I say. 'That's no ordinary litter. That's our way off this island.'

'It is?' says Jill.

'Yes,' I say. 'We can put a message in a bottle! It's what everybody who's marooned on a desert island does!'

'Did you say *message in a bottle*?' says Terry. 'I love message-in-a-bottle bottles!'

'Me too,' says Alice.

'Me three!' says Albert.

'Me four,' I say. I grab a piece of driftpaper and a driftpencil and start writing a driftletter.

Andy, Terry, Jill, Alice, Albert & the baby
Desert Island
The Ocean
The Middle of Nowhere

Dear Whoever You Are,

If you are like most of the people who find a bottle with a message inside it, you're probably wondering what the message is about. Well, it contains a long and tragic story. Which is this: unfortunately me (Andy) and my friends (Terry & Jill) and the kids we are babysitting (Albert & Alice & the baby) have accidentally become marooned on a desert island. Could you please organise a rescue mission to come and rescue us as soon as possible?

Thank you (in advance).

Your pals,
Andy, Terry, Jill, Alice, Albert & the baby

I roll up the message, slide it into the bottle and hand it to Terry. He plugs the end with a driftcork and throws it as far out into the water as he can, and then we all immediately start waiting for a reply.

We wait …

and we wait …

and we wait …

149

until finally, after what seems like *millions* of pages but is in fact only one-and-a-half, we see a bottle floating towards us.

'Hey, look!' says Terry. 'A message in a bottle!'

'YAY!' says Albert.

Terry runs into the water to retrieve it.

'How exciting!' says Jill. 'Who do you think it's from?'

'From whoever found our message in a bottle, of course!' I say. 'It's probably got all the details of how they're going to rescue us.'

Terry uncorks the bottle and shakes the message free.

'It's from some people just like us,' he says, 'same names and everything—and they're marooned on a desert island too!'

'Terry,' I say.

'Hang on, Andy,' he says, 'I haven't finished reading the letter. It says here they need help.'

'I know,' I say.

'How?'

'Because it's *us*!' I say. 'It's *our* bottle and *our* letter! It just floated away and then floated back again.'

'Hmmm,' says Jill. 'And maybe the bottle just floated away and then came back because this desert island is *your* desert island?'

'What do you mean *our* desert island?' I say.

'The new desert island level in your treehouse,' says Jill.

'Oh yeah,' I say. 'I forgot we had one.'

'Well, there's an easy way to find out if that's where we are,' says Jill. 'We can climb that tree and look.'

153

It *is* our desert island!
We've been in
the treehouse
the whole
time!

Terry reaches up for a vine that is
hanging above us. 'Grab on to this,'
he says, 'and we can all
swing up to the next level.'

'Wheeeeee!' says Alice, as we swing through the air.

'I love swinging!' says Albert.

'Goo-goo ga-ga!' says the baby.

We land in the kitchen.

'I'm glad we're all safe again,' says Jill. 'I've got to go home now and feed my animals, but I'll come back as soon as I can to help you with the babysitting. In the meantime, keep a close eye on Alice, Albert and the baby. And, whatever you do, *don't* let them out of your sight!'

'Don't worry about that, Jill,' I say. 'We've learned our lesson: I'm going to draw up a babysitting roster so that one of us is watching them at *all times*.'

'Great idea,' says Jill. 'See you later.'

'What are we going to do while you do the roster?' says Alice.

'Here's a colour-by-numbers colouring-in sheet I prepared earlier,' says Terry.

'Yay!' says Albert. 'I *love* colouring in!'

The kids start colouring in and Terry and I get started on our roster. (You can colour in the picture, too, readers, if you would like.)

'I think we should take turns looking after the kids,' I say. 'How about I do the first five minutes and then I take a ten-minute break and while I'm on my break you watch them for ten minutes and then you take a five-minute break and then we just repeat that pattern until we're done.'

'But that's not fair,' says Terry. 'You're only working five minutes at a time and taking ten-minute breaks, and I'm working ten minutes at a time and only getting five-minute breaks.'

'Oops,' I say. 'My mistake. What about we each work for five minutes and each take ten-minute breaks?'

'It's better—and fairer—than the first roster,' says Terry, 'but it means we won't get to spend much time together.'

'Hmmm,' I say. 'Let me see. I know! Perhaps we could do our first five minutes at the same time and then we can take our breaks together.'

'Perfect!' says Terry. 'You're really good at rosters, Andy.'

'Thanks,' I say. 'Let's get started right away.'

'Kids!' says Terry. 'Andy's done a really good roster. We're ready to start babysitting now … um … kids? Kids? Andy—they're gone!'

'Oh, no!' I say. 'Not again! If only they'd waited until we'd finished our roster this would never have happened! Let's go straight to Madam Know-it-all and find out where they are before they get into trouble again.'

We climb the tree as fast as we can and burst into Madam Know-it-all's tent.

'Aha,' she says, 'I knew—'

'There's no time for that!' I say. 'Please tell us where the kids are—and if you could skip the cryptic rhyme we'd really appreciate it. We're in kind of a hurry.'

'I know,' sighs Madam Know-it-all.

I know you don't have time.
But I always do a rhyme.
So here's your cryptic clue:
MARBAGE MUMP—pee-uw!

'*Barbage bump?*' I say.

'No,' she says.

'*Farbage frump?*'
says Terry.

'No,' she says.

'*Zarbage zump?*' I say.

'Oh, for goodness' sake,' says Madam Know-it-all. 'It's GARBAGE DUMP, you dumdums! The kids are at the garbage dump!'

CHAPTER 7

Banarnia

Terry and I hurry to the garbage dump and start climbing.

'I love the dump,' says Terry. 'You never know what you're going to find.'

'Well, I hope we find Mr Big Nose's grandchildren,' I say. 'That's what we're here for, remember?'

'Oh yeah,' says Terry. 'I forgot. Hey, look what I found! It's a medal! It says WORLD'S GREATEST DA.'

'What's a DA?' I say.

'I don't know,' says Terry, putting it around his neck, 'but whatever it is, I'm the greatest one in the world!'

'Congratulations, Terry,' I say, 'but you'll be a dead
DA if we don't find those kids.'

'Good point, Andy,' says Terry. 'Alice! Albert!
Where are you?'

I see a little face peering out of the garbage.

'Terry!' I call. 'I've found the baby!'

I reach into the rubbish, grab hold of the baby and
pull it towards me.

But it's not the baby! It's a telephone with a cute
little face.

'That's not the baby!' says Terry.

'Well I know that *now*!' I say. 'But it looked like the baby when it was buried in rubbish and all I could see was its cute little face.'

'Never mind,' says Terry. 'Look on the bright side: at least now you've got a telephone with a cute little face.'

'Yes,' I say, 'and when you pull it along its eyes go up and down, see?'

'That is SO cool!' says Terry.

RING RING!
RING RING!
RING RING!

'And listen to that,' I say. 'It rings too.'

'I think you should answer it,' says Terry.

I pick up the receiver.

'Hello, is that Andy?' says a voice.

'Yes,' I say. 'Who is this?'

'It's Mrs Big Nose here,' says the voice. 'It's half-time at the opera and I just thought I'd check in and see how the children are. Everything going well?'

'Um … good,' I say. 'Really good. Really, really, really good.'

'Well … er … um … no,' I say. 'Not right at the moment.'

'Can I talk to them?' says Mrs Big Nose.

'No?' she says. 'Why not?'

'Well … because … um … we're sort of playing hide-and-seek and it's their turn to hide.'

'Oh, lovely,' says Mrs Big Nose. 'I won't disturb them, then. I know how much they love their hide-and-seek. Sounds like you boys are doing a great job. Here's a little hint for you—their favourite place to hide is in wardrobes. Goodbye.'

She hangs up.

'Who was that?' says Terry.

'Mrs Big Nose,' I say. 'She was just calling to see how the kids were and she said their favourite place to hide is in wardrobes.'

'Look!' says Terry. 'There's a wardrobe at the top of the garbage pile. Come on!'

We scramble up to the top of the pile as fast as we can. There's laughter coming from inside the wardrobe.

'They're definitely in there!' says Terry.

'Found you!' I say, flinging the doors of the wardrobe wide open. Except we haven't, because they're not here. The wardrobe is empty.

'I can't see them,' says Terry, 'but I can still *hear* them. That's *weird*.'

'I think I know what's going on here,' I say. 'This is no *ordinary* wardrobe. This is a *storybook* wardrobe. It's most likely one of those portals to another world—like the wardrobe that leads to Narnia in *The Lion, the Witch and the Wardrobe*.'

'I *love* portals!' says Terry, climbing into the wardrobe. 'Come on!'

I follow Terry into the storybook wardrobe, pulling my new phone with the cute little face behind me.

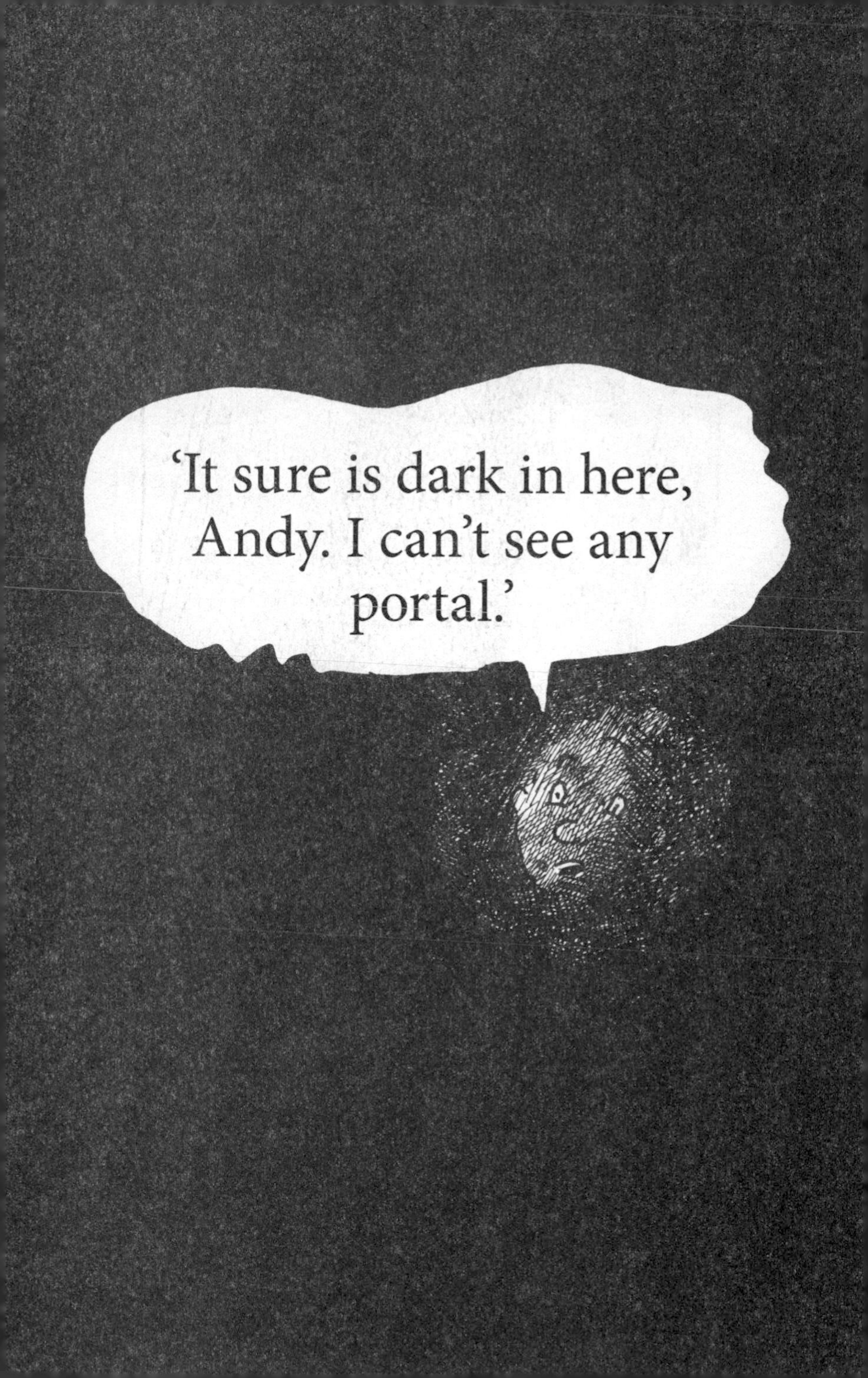
'It sure is dark in here, Andy. I can't see any portal.'

‘This *is* the portal, you idiot! Keep going. There’s light up ahead …’

'Wow, this place is bananas!' says Terry.

'Yeah,' I say. 'It's not like Narnia at all. It's more like *BAnarnia*!'

'You're right about that,' says Terry. 'There are flying toasters and walking cars. And, look, there's Alice and Albert and the baby—they're riding ... well, I don't know what they're called ... but they're riding them.'

'Come here!' I yell. 'And get off those whatever-they-ares. Terry and I will be in big trouble if anything happens to you!'

'But we're having fun!' Alice yells back.

'Yeah!' calls Albert. 'Try and catch us!'

'Goo-goo ga-ga!' says the baby, as they speed off into the distance.

BOING! BOING! BOING!

Terry and I each grab a whatever-they're-called and take off after them.

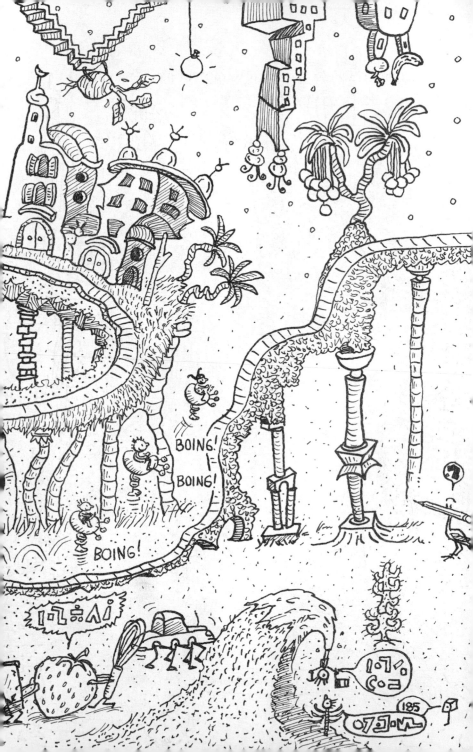

BOING! BOING! BOING!

IIOOIL

A big duck →

187

The kids are right. Riding these things *is* fun.
Until we all come to the edge of a big cliff, that is.

Our whatever-you-call-thems stop ... but we don't.
We are flung forward over the edge.

Uh-oh!

We all fall down ...

and down ...

and down ...

CHAPTER 8

Stuck!

'What are we going to do, Andy?' says Terry.

'Prepare for a crash landing,' I say.

'That sounds painful,' says Terry.

'Got any better ideas?' I say.

'Flap your arms,' calls Albert.

'Yes,' says Alice. 'Look, we can fly!'

I look up. It's true—the kids are flying!

Terry and I start flapping our arms ...

and soon we stop falling … and start flying too!

Whoosh!

Wheeee!

Zoom!

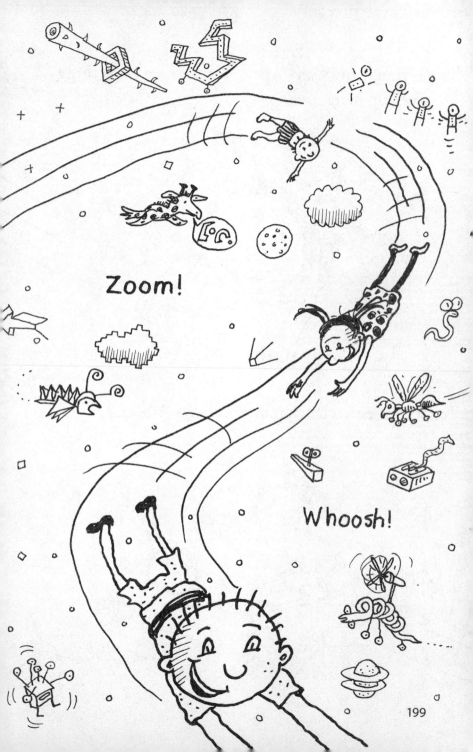

Zoom!

Whoosh!

'Flying is fun!' says Alice. 'You can see everything from up here!'

'I can see a whatchamacallit!' says Albert.

'And there's a thingummybob!' says Terry.

'I can see a whirly thing!' I say. 'It's going round and round and round and it's heading straight for us!'

'Oh, goody,' says Alice. 'Whirly things are fun.'

'I wouldn't be so sure of that,' I say. 'Not *all* whirly things are fun. This looks like one of those dangerous sort of whirly things that knocks down trees, picks up houses, sucks people up and is called … um … I can't remember what they're called, but I think it starts with "t".'

'Tomato?' says Terry.

'Yes!' I say. 'A tomato! And it's headed this way!'

'It's not a tomato,' says Albert. 'It's a tornado!'

'Phew!' says Terry. 'For a moment there I thought we were in trouble.'

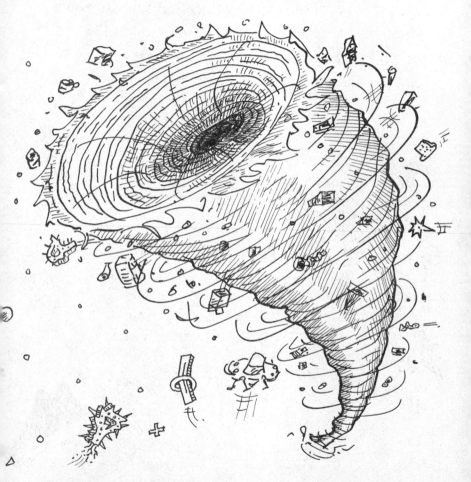

'We *are* in trouble,' I say. '*Serious* trouble—this is going to get rough!'

The tomato sucks us all up and we are whirled and twirled and spun and then spat out. We fly through the air and land in a soft, springy net.

It's a bit sticky, which makes it hard to move, but it's much more relaxing than being whirled around in a tomato.

There's a big black thing in the net with us. It's got a lot of legs and is quite hairy. I'm pretty sure I know what this is called. It starts with 's'. It's a … sss … a sss …

'Spy cow!' says Terry.

'Where?!' I say.

'Over there!' says Terry, pointing to the big black thing.

'That's not a *spy cow*,' says Alice. 'That's a spider!'

'That's it! *Spider!*' I say. 'We're stuck in a giant spider web!'

'What are we going to do?' says Terry.

'Call Jill,' says Albert. 'That's what you always do when you have problems—especially animal ones.'

'Who's Jill?' I say.

'She's your friend,' says Alice. 'She lives next door.'

'She does?' I say. 'Never heard of her.'

'I can't believe you don't remember Jill,' says Albert. 'What about you, Terry? You remember her, don't you?'

'Terry?' says Terry. 'Who's Terry?'

'*You* are!' says Alice. '*You're* Terry. Andy's friend.'

'Who's Andy?' I say.

'Uh-oh,' says Alice. 'I think *I'd* better call Jill.'

Alice picks up the phone and dials.

'Hello, Jill?' she says. 'It's Alice.'

'Hello, Alice!' says Jill. 'How are you?'

'Good, thanks!' says Alice. 'Well … except that we're all stuck in a giant spider web.'

'What?! Spider web?! What are you doing in a spider web?'

'Well, we were playing on the garbage dump and then we went into an old wardrobe and we found a strange land where we could fly and then we were flying around and we got sucked up into a giant tornado and then we ended up here.'

'Are Andy and
Terry with you?'

'Yes. But there's
something wrong
with them. They've
forgotten who they
are. They've even
forgotten who
you are!'

'Oh dear. What is
wrong with those
two? They've become
so forgetful lately!'

'I know! They can't even remember what things are called. Andy called the tornado a tomato and Terry thought the spider was a spy cow!'

'Don't worry, Alice. I'm on my way. Can you and Albert look after Andy and Terry and the baby till I get there?'

'Yes, but please hurry. I don't like spiders.'

'Cool!' says Albert. 'Now *we're* the babysitters! And *they're* the babies.'

CHAPTER 9

Smarter and Smarterer

Hi, readers, it's Jill here. As you know, something's gone wrong with Andy and Terry so I'm going to narrate for a little while until we can fix them … Oh, look at that amazing butterfly—

it's a brush-footed, gossamer-winged loop-the-looper, if I'm not mistaken. Yep, look at those loops! It's the loopiest insect in the whole animal kingdom—capable of up to one million loops per day!

The only other insect to come close to that is the somersaulting silverfish of Soweto—

which reminds me of a funny story—

'Jill,' says Alice. 'You're supposed to be narrating the book, not talking about animals.'

'Oh, sorry,' I say. 'I got completely distracted by the loop-the-looper.'

Now where was I? Oh, that's right. At the end of the last chapter, I rescued Andy, Terry, Alice, Albert and the baby from the giant spider web in the treehouse.

Silky and her flying cat friends helped to bring everybody back to my house, which is where we are now.

'What's wrong with Andy and Terry?' says Albert.

'Well,' I say, 'let's see, shall we?'

I shine a torch into Andy's right ear.

The beam of light passes through his head and comes out his left ear and then travels into Terry's right ear, through his head, and out the other side.

'Ah, I see the problem,' I say. 'Their heads are completely empty. It's as if their brains have been drained of all knowledge.'

'Oh no!' says Alice. 'What are you going to do?'

'Fill them up again, of course!' I say. 'Luckily I have an early learning centre for animals. I opened it just last week.'

'But Andy and Terry aren't *animals*!' says Alice.

'Yes they are,' I say. 'They're *human* animals ... we all are! And right now I need you both to be human animal teachers. You're going to help me re-educate Andy and Terry. Let's take them to the early learning centre.'

222

223

I go to my shelf of learn to read books. I have one
for each animal, including Andy and Terry.

'Who would
like to read this
one to them?'
I say.

'I will,' says
Albert.

He opens the
book and starts
reading.

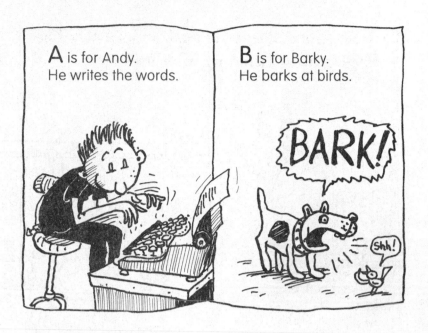

A is for Andy.
He writes the words.

B is for Barky.
He barks at birds.

BARK!

Shh!

C is for clones.
They helped
build the ramp.

D is for drawing.
Terry's the champ!

E is for egg.
A giant unhatched one.

F is for friends.
They play and they
have fun.

G is for gorilla.
The biggest in the land.

H is for Hee-Haw.
He bit Terry's hand.

I is for ice-cream.
There are flavours galore.

TUM!

J is for Jill.
She lives next door.

ANDY! TERRY!

K is for Kevin.
The mechanical bull.

L is for lemonade.
You can drink till
you're full.

GLUG! SLURP!

M is for Mr Big Nose.
He likes to shout.

N is for Ninja Snails.
They once helped
you out.

O is for owls.
'Wise' things they
proclaim.

P is for postman.
Bill is his name.

U is for underpants.
Terry's can inflate.

V is for vegetables,
which you really,
really hate.

W is for watermelons.
Smash! Smash! Smash!

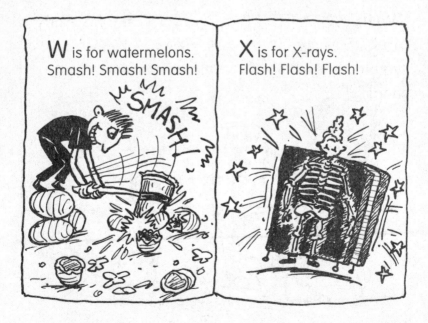

X is for X-rays.
Flash! Flash! Flash!

Y is for you, the reader. (That's *you* and *you* and *you*!)

And Z is for the ama-Z-ing baby dinosaur petting zoo!

'Well done, Albert,' I say. 'Now it's time for Andy and Terry to learn their numbers. Alice, would you like to read them this treehouse counting book?'

'Yes, please, Jill,' she says. 'I *love* numbers.'

Six letters

Seven penguins

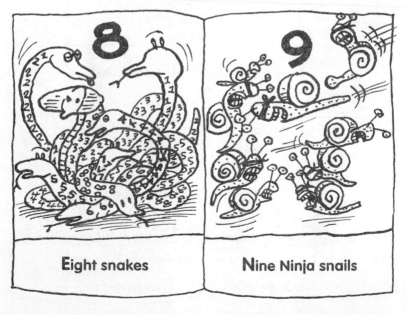

Eight snakes

Nine Ninja snails

10

Ten Andys

11 Yuk!

Brussel Sprouts

Eleven brussel sprouts

12

Twelve cats

13 Rabbits Rule.

Thirteen rabbits

'Good work!' I say. 'Now they've got the basics, it's time to put the rest of their knowledge back in. Time to sing my *Everything there is to know about everything* song!'

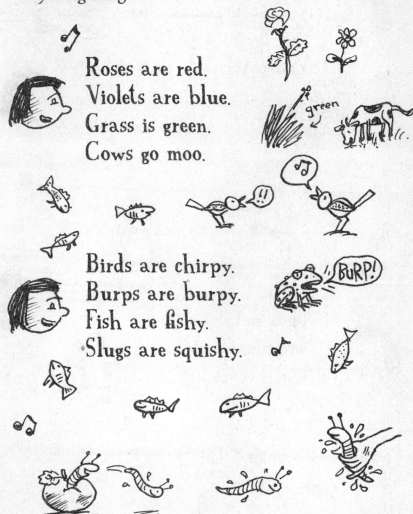

Roses are red.
Violets are blue.
Grass is green.
Cows go moo.

Birds are chirpy.
Burps are burpy.
Fish are fishy.
Slugs are squishy.

Water is wet
And so is sweat.
You fly in a jet.
And catch fish in a net.

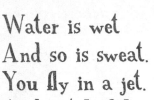

Fire is hot.
Ice is not.
Penguins waddle
And horses trot.

A square has four sides,
A triangle three.
A circle has one:
It's as round as can be.

Sticks are thin.
Logs are thick.
Dogs can bite
And run quite quick.

Mice are small.
Giraffes are tall.
Worms are wriggly.
Squiggles are squiggly.

Bikes are for riding.
Slides are for sliding.
Caves are for hiding.
Stick & dots (÷) for dividing.

Hands are for waving.
Feet are for walking.
Mouths are for eating
And also for talking.

Eyes are for seeing
And blinking and winking.
Ears are for hearing
And brains are for thinking.

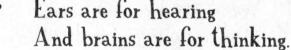

You can live in a cottage
A hutch or a nest.
An igloo is cool
But a treehouse is best.

A hat is a thing
You wear on your head.
A rat is a thing
You don't want in your bed.

The sky is up.
The ground is down.
Clouds are white.
And dirt is brown.

Brown

white

OUCH!

DO..RE..
ME..SO..
FA...
etc

Tops are for spinning
And knobs are for turning.
Songs are for singing
And sometimes for learning!

TRA-LAAAA!

241

♪ Some songs are short
But this one is long ♪
Because it's the Everything-
there-is-to-know-about-
everything song! ♫

'Wasn't that fun?' I say.

'Yes,' says Terry. 'And *very* educational!
I feel *much* smarter now.'

'Me too,' says Andy. 'I bet I'm much more
smarterer than you!'

'No way,' says Terry. 'I'm a *million billion* times smarterer than you!'

'Are not!' says Andy. 'I'm a *million billion frillion* times smarterer than you!'

'No you're not,' says Terry. 'I'm a million billion frillion … (yawn) gillion hillion jillion nillion … (yawn, yawn) quillion spillion trillion willion xillion yillion … (yawn yawn yawn) zillionzzzzzzzzzzzzzzzzzzzzzzzzzzzzz …'

'Look!' says Alice. 'Terry fell asleep while he was *talking*.'

'And Andy fell asleep while he was *listening*!' says Albert.

'They must be tired after all that learning,' I say. 'Not to mention all that boasting.'

'So are they back to normal now?' says Alice.

'Almost,' I say. 'But they're nowhere near as smart as they *think* they are. We'll have to put some more knowledge into their ears while they're asleep.'

FALSE FACTS

True facts

MECHANICAL ENGINEERING FACTS PLUS TRIVIA

MATHS

Emotional Facts

Building skills

SCIENCE

WEIRD FACTS

It's okay. They don't use that!

LOGIC

'Okay, I think we're done,' I say. 'Let's do the torch test again.'

This time when I shine a light into Andy's ear it doesn't pass through.

'Their brains are full to the brim!' I say.

'Yay!' say Alice and Albert.

'I think we should all have a little rest now,' I say. 'Andy will be able to take over the narration again when he wakes up.'

It's been really fun being your emergency narrator—thanks for being such great readers and listeners!

CHAPTER 10

WARNING!

Greetings, dear reader! My name is Andrew.
I am your humble narrator and—along with
Terence Denton—the co-creator of the Treehouse
Chronicles, which is a full and honest account of
our lives in a unique elevated dwelling.

If you show a kinship to the majority of our readership—that is to say, if you are possessed of a lively spirit and an inquiring mind—you may, perchance, have found yourself pondering the reasons for my—and Terence's—frequent lapses of memory during the course of the preceding pages.

'Hey, Andy!' says Terence.

'Not now, Terence,' I say. 'I am currently engaged in a matter of the utmost narratorial urgency and must not be interrupted under any circumstances.'

'But—' says Terence.

'I am terribly sorry,' I say, 'but I really must insist that you refrain from these irrelevant interjections that threaten the great and important enterprise I am currently embarked upon.'

'But—' splutters Terence.

'What is the matter with you today, Terence?'
I say. 'Do you not have sufficient intellectual
faculties to comprehend plain English?'

'*Plain* English I *can* understand,' says Terence.
'But I *can't* understand a single other word you just
said and I don't think our readers can either.'

'Poppycock and fiddlesticks!' I say. 'I will have you know my multi-syllabic narrative powers are without comparison in the realms of literary endeavour and my works are admired across the entire universe by civilisations both known and yet to be discovered. There are more things in heaven and earth, Terence, than are dreamt of in your philosophy.'

'I don't know what you're talking about,' says
Terence. 'But it sounds like you swallowed
a dictionary for breakfast. And for your
information, my name is Terry, not *Terence*!'

'Actually, I think you will find that in actual fact
Terry is an abbreviation of both *Terrance* and
Terrell. It is also an Anglicised phonetic form of
the French given name *Thierry*, a Norman French
form of *Theodoric* from an older Germanic name
meaning "small-brained one".'

'What's wrong with Andy?' says Alice.

'I don't know,' says Albert. 'I can't understand him any more.'

'Neither can I,' says Jill. 'I think we've made him *too* smart for his own good!'

'Don't worry,' says Terence. 'I know exactly what he needs. I'll be right back.'

And with that, Terence departs with great alacrity.

Barely a moment elapses before Terence reappears, bearing aloft an enormous mallet.

'Hold still, Andy,' he says. 'This won't hurt a bit. Well, when I say it won't hurt a bit I mean, obviously, it will hurt a *lot*, so here goes …'

'Is he all right?' says Alice.

'I'll check,' says Terence. He shakes my shoulder. 'Say something, Andy!'

'Um … er … ah … the sum of the square roots of any two sides of an isosceles triangle is equal to the square root of the remaining side.'

'Sounds like he might need another donk,' says Terence.

I open my eyes.

Terry studies me closely. 'What's two plus two?' he says.

'Um ... five?' I say.

'Yay!' says Terry. 'You're back to normal!'

'Thanks, Terry,' I say. 'I needed that. Being a super genius brainiac is exhausting.'

'Don't thank me,' he says. 'Thank Jill and the kids for filling our brains back up. Something must have happened to them in Banarnia.'

'I don't think it was Banarnia that caused the problem,' says Jill. 'Alice, Albert and the baby went there too and they didn't forget everything they knew. And don't forget that both of you were forgetting other stuff *before* you went to Banarnia.'

'Oh, yeah,' I say. 'I forgot. But if it wasn't Banarnia that caused our brain meltdowns then what was it?'

Before we can figure it out, however, Jill's rooster doorbell rings.

Jill's animals react immediately. Laika and Loompy bark. Pat moos. Bill and Phil bounce around like superballs. Larry, Curly and Mo look up from their card game and the excited rabbits hop around like a bunch of excited rabbits.

Jill answers the door.

It's Bill the postman!

We all say hello and the animals crowd around him.

'Good morning,' says Bill. 'I'm here on official poster posting business. The Forest Police Department wanted these WARNING posters put up. A dangerous fortune teller has escaped from a maximum-security travelling carnival. Apparently, she's a brain-drainer.'

We walk out into the forest. Bill really has been busy. He has put a poster on every single tree!

WARNING

DANGEROUS FORTUNE TELLER ON THE LOOSE!

WHATEVER YOU DO, DO **NOT** ASK HER ANY QUESTIONS OR SHE WILL DRAIN EVERY LAST DROP OF KNOWLEDGE FROM YOUR BRAIN.

THE MORE YOU ASK
THE LESS YOU'LL KNOW
YOUR BRAIN WILL SHRINK
WHILE HERS WILL GROW!

DO NOT INVITE HER TO SET UP HER TENT IN YOUR COTTAGE, BURROW, BARN, STABLE, HUTCH OR TREEHOUSE, OR YOU WILL BE VERY, VERY, VERY SORRY!

An Official Forest Police Department Publication
—Keeping your forest safe since 2011—

'Yikes!' says Terry. 'She sounds dangerous.'

'She is!' says Bill. 'Have any of you seen her?'

'No,' I say. 'But thanks for the warning, Bill. We'll certainly keep our eyes open.'

'All right,' says Bill, 'but if you do see her, whatever you do, don't ask her any questions or she'll drain your brains. See you all later!'

We wave goodbye to Bill and watch as Jill's animals race alongside his scooter till he's out of view.

BARK!

Giraffe noise!

'Maybe we should have told Bill about Madam Know-it-all,' I say. 'She might be able to help the authorities track down that evil fortune teller. After all, she *does* know everything.'

'Wait a minute,'
says Terry.

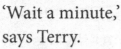

'WAIT a minute …
Hang on …

Just another
minute …

I'VE GOT IT!
Prepare yourself for
some shocking news …
The dangerous brain-
draining fortune teller
who is on the loose is
none other than …

'Of course!' I say. 'That's why we've been forgetting everything. Madam Know-it-all drained our brains!'

'Oh, no!' says Terry. 'And now that our brains have been refilled she'll drain them again!'

'Calm down, you two,' says Jill. 'Remember what the poster said. She can only drain your brain if you ask her questions. So don't ask her any questions and you'll be fine.'

'But how are we going to get her out of the treehouse?' I say.

'We could ask her to leave,' says Terry.

'But that's a *question*,' I say.

'Oh yeah,' says Terry. 'Good point, Andy.'

'I think you should just *tell* her to leave,' says Jill. 'Just say you're really sorry but you made a mistake and you need the level for something else. My animals and I will all come with you. Just remember, whatever you do, *don't ask her any questions*!'

CHAPTER 11

The Turbanator!

We all pile into Jill's flying cat sleigh and fly straight to the treehouse.

We land on Madam Know-it-all's level.

'You go in first,' I say to Terry, pushing him forward.

'No, I'm scared,' he says, slipping behind me and pushing *me* towards the tent flap. '*You* go in first.'

'I've got a better idea,' I say. 'Let's make the *animals* go in first!'

'Good thinking,' says Terry. 'Give me a hand with Manny, Andy!'

We're pushing Manny into the tent but Jill stops us. 'Andy and Terry!' she says. 'Stop pushing my goat!'

'But Terry pushed *me*,' I say.

'Andy pushed me first,' says Terry.

'Two wrongs don't make a right—and they certainly don't make a good reason to push goats!' says Jill. 'How about we all go in together?'

'I've got a better idea,' says Madam Know-it-all, emerging from her tent. 'How about *I* come out since there are so many of you?'

'Madam Know-it-all!' gasps Terry in surprise.

'Yes, it is I, Madam Know-it-all. I know all and see all,' she says. 'I believe you have something you wish to ask me?'

'Well, as a matter of fact we *do*,' says Terry. 'Would you—'

I clamp my hand across Terry's mouth.

'We didn't come to ask you anything,' I say. 'We came to *tell* you something. We came to tell you to leave.'

'Immediately,' says Jill.

Alice and Albert nod their heads.

'Goo-goo ga-ga,' says the baby.

'Why don't you *ask* me to leave?' says Madam
Know-it-all. 'That would be more polite.'

'No,' I say. 'We're not asking you any more
questions *ever*!'

'Oh,' says Madam Know-it-all with a sly smile. 'I see. So you're telling me there's *nothing* more you want to know.'

'That's correct,' I say. 'Nothing.'

'Not even whether you're going to get this book written on time?'

'I know we'll get our book written on time,' I say. 'We always do—somehow.'

'Very well, then,' says Madam Know-it-all. 'What about *you*, Terry? Wouldn't you like to know what your eyebrows taste like? I *know* you've often wondered! All you have to do is to ask me.'

'Yes, I *have* wondered,' says Terry. 'Quite often, actually. But I'm not going to ask you.' He shakes his head and then clamps his hands over his mouth just to make sure.

'Suit yourself,' says Madam Know-it-all. 'What about you, Jill? Wouldn't you like to know what my snakes' names are?'

'No,' says Jill, 'because I've made up my own names for them—Slidey, Slithery and Roger.'

'Those *are* their names!' says Madam Know-it-all, looking surprised. 'But wouldn't you like to know their ssssurnames?'

'Snakes don't have surnames,' says Jill. 'That's just silly!'

Madam Know-it-all shrugs and turns her attention to the kids.

'What about you, Alice? Wouldn't you like to know what you're going to be when you grow up?'

'I already know,' says Alice. 'I'm going to be like Jill and live in a house full of animals.'

'And I'm going to be just like Terry and live in a treehouse and draw cool pictures!' says Albert.

'Hey!' I say. 'How come nobody wants to be like *me* when they grow up?'

STOP THAT!

'Is that a question?' says Madam Know-it-all.

'Not for *you*, it's not,' I say.

'All right,' says Madam Know-it-all. 'If none of you are going to ask me any questions, then you leave me no choice but to unleash … *The Turbanator!*'

She pushes the jewel on the front of her turban
and dozens of tubes—each with a little turban on
the end—spring out of the top.

'Run!' I say.

RING
RING

We run, but it's no use. The mini-turbans rain down from above and wrap themselves around our heads. We're all wrapped and trapped—even the kids and all of Jill's animals.

We try to pull the turbans off, but they won't budge.

'There's no use struggling,' says Madam Know-it-all. 'The Turbanator is a multi-brain-draining machine. Once activated it will drain your brains into mine. The turbans will not release until your heads are completely empty.'

'Please don't drain our brains again,' says Terry.

'Oh, but thanks to Jill, they're filled to the brim with even more facts and information than before,' says Madam Know-it-all. 'I simply can't resist!'

'But *why*?' pleads Jill. 'You already know everything—or so you claim. What more could you possibly want to know? What more could there even *be* to know?'

'Ah,' sighs Madam Know-it-all. 'How *little* you know about how *much* there is to know! You see, the more you know, the more you know how much there is that you *don't* know. And I'm not going to rest until I know every last thing there is to know in the entire world.'

'Huh?' says Jill.

'It might be simpler if I sing it for you,' says Madam Know-it-all. And so she does.

I WANT TO KNOW EVERYTHING
(as sung by Madam Know-it-all)

I know more than Google,
Yahoo and Wikipedia,
For I am Madam Know-it-all,
The human encyclopaedia!

But don't tell me that I know enough
Because I know I never will.
The thought of all I still don't know
Makes me feel rather ill.

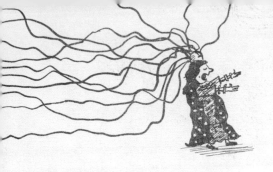

I want to know who and what
And why and when and how.
I want to know it all
And I want to know it now.

I want to know who made the colours
And gave each one a name.
And who the heck made spiders?
Is there someone we can blame?

288

I want to know why flowers grow,
Why rivers flow and noses blow.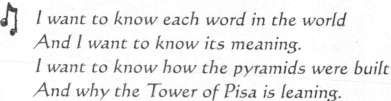
I want to know where rainbows go.
I really, really want to know!

I want to know each word in the world
And I want to know its meaning.
I want to know how the pyramids were built
And why the Tower of Pisa is leaning.

I want to know why volcanoes erupt
And how mountains rise and fall.
I want to know the price of fish.
I want to know it ALL!

I want to know why rocks are hard
And cookies always crumble.
I want to know why babies laugh
And old men like to grumble.

I want to know hither
And I want to know thither.
I want to know the difference
Between xylophone and zither.

Who made typewriters?
Who made the moon?
How many black rings
On the tail of a raccoon?

Who's the fastest? Who's the tallest?
Who's the strongest and the best?
Who's the richest? Who's the poorest?
Which bird builds the biggest nest?
What's the widest? What's the deepest?
Why does the sun set in the west?
Until I know it all,
I will never, ever rest!

CHAPTER 12

Pop-Pop Pops!

'The video phone is ringing,' says Terry.
'I know!' says Madam Know-it-all.

'You should answer it,' I say. 'It will probably be Mr Big Nose!'

'I know!' says Madam Know-it-all.

'He probably wants Alice and Albert and the baby back,' says Terry.

'I know,' says Madam Know-it-all.

'You really should answer it,' I say. 'He doesn't like to be kept waiting.'

'I know!' says Madam Know-it-all.

Madam Know-it-all answers the phone. Mr Big
Nose's face—and nose—fills the screen.

'Hello!' he yells. 'It's Mr Big Nose here!'
  'I know who you are,' says Madam Know-it-all.

'I want to speak to Andy and Terry.'

'I know that too,' says Madam Know-it-all.

'Then put them on,' he says. 'I'm a very busy man, you know.'

'I know,' she says.

'Put them on at once,' he says. 'I'm getting impatient.'

'I know you are,' says Madam Know-it-all.

'I've had just about enough of this,' he says.

'I know you have,' she says. 'I am Madam Know-it-all and I know *everything*. Is there anything you'd like to know? All you have to do is ask.'

'Well, listen up, Madam Whoever-you-are,' says
Mr Big Nose. 'Here's something you don't know: if
you don't stop wasting my time and put Andy and
Terry on the phone I'm going to get *very* angry!'
  'Actually, I *do* know that,' says Madam Know-it-all.

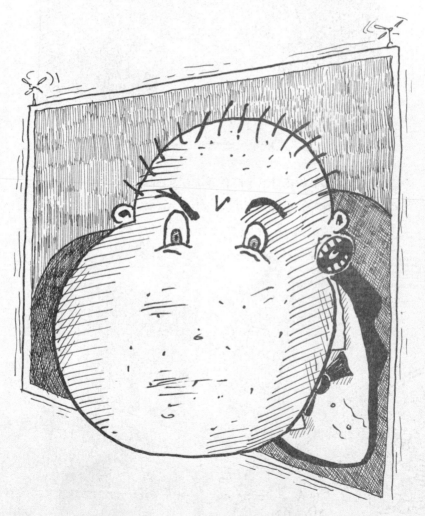

'I can't take much more of this,' he says. 'You are pushing me to the limit of my patience!'

'I know I am,' says Madam Know-it-all.

'You're making me very, VERY angry!' he says.

'I know,' she says.

'In fact, I'm so angry I feel like I could explode ...
or a certain part of me, at least.'

'I know,' she says.

'Uh-oh,' I say.
　　'Uh-oh,' says Terry.
　　'Uh-oh,' says Jill.

305

The force of the explosion sends us all flying
backwards.

We sit up and look at each other.

'Is everybody okay?' says Jill.

'I think I am,' says Alice.

'Me too,' says Albert.

'Pop-pop's nose go pop!' says the baby.

We all laugh.

'Hey!' says Terry, patting his head. 'The brain-draining turbans are gone!'

'And so is Madam Know-it-all,' I say. 'Look!'

In the place where Madam Know-it-all was standing, there is only a pair of smoking shoes and three stunned snakes.

'Eeek! Snakes!' says Terry.
  'Oh, you poor things,' says Jill, picking them up.

'Be careful, Jill,' I say. 'They're evil fortune teller's snakes!'

'No they're not,' says Jill, cuddling them close to her face. 'You're just innocent victims, aren't you? Would you like to come and live with me in my cottage?'

The snakes hiss excitedly, which I guess means yes. Jill's other animals aren't looking quite as enthusiastic, though.

'Do you think Pop-pop's nose will be all right?' says Albert.

'Yes,' I say. 'It's probably not the first time it's happened ... and, somehow, I doubt it will be the last.'

'Now that Madam Know-it-all is gone,' says Alice. 'What will you do with her tent?'

'We could turn this level into a campsite,' I say.

'Yeah,' says Terry. 'It would be fun to camp out every now and then and have a campfire.'

'I've got an idea,' says Jill. 'You could create a
Madam Know-it-all memorial reference library
and fill it with proper reference books, full of true
facts and accurate information.'

'What about fiction?' says Terry. 'Can our library
have books with made-up stuff, too?'

'Yes, of course,' says Jill. 'You can learn from fiction as well as from non-fiction.'

'Quite right, Jill,' I say. 'It's my considered opinion that knowledge is power, but there is a limit to what we can know and what we can learn in this lifetime, so it's important to let our imaginations run wild and set us free, because imagination is the force that can unlock the power within and give us what knowledge cannot.'

'Do I need to get my mallet again, Andy?' says Terry.

'No,' I say. 'I'm sorry about that. I have no idea what I just said but think I'm okay now.'

That reminds me... I must buy some more fish!

'I think what's important here,' says Jill, 'is that if you want to know stuff, just read a book—any book for goodness' sake. There's no need to go around turbanating other people's brains!'

'Speaking of books,' I say, 'we still haven't written ours!'

'Can we be in it?' says Alice.

'Yes, please put us in the book,' says Albert. 'I've always wanted to be a character in a book. Especially one of yours!'

'Of course you can be in it!' I say. 'In fact, you can even help us write and draw it!'

'Yay!' says Albert. 'But what will the story be about?'

'Babysitting, of course!' says Terry.

'Yeah!' says Alice. 'We'll call it *The Funnest and Best Babysitting Day Ever!*'

'Well, that is a great title,' I say, 'but I think we'd probably better call it *The 91-Storey Treehouse* or our readers might get confused.'

'Okay,' says Alice. '*The 91-Storey Treehouse* it is.'

CHAPTER 13

The Last Chapter

We all set to work as fast as we can.

We write …

and we draw …

'No,' says Mr Big Nose, 'that's *Pinocchio*—just a silly children's story. I'm talking about opera—*serious* opera. *Il Bignosio d' Explodio* speaks of matters far above your heads. Art, truth, beauty, exploding noses ... in fact, it starts with the most explosive operatic aria of all time! Here, I'll sing it for you.'

Oh my big no se-io! The crosser! get-io,

The bigger it grows-io, Then it **BOOM CRASH EXPLODES-IO!**

52

53

and we draw ...

SINK -O- METER®

1000 LEAGUES
2000 LEAGUES
3000 LEAGUES
4000 LEAGUES
5000 LEAGUES
6000 LEAGUES
7000 LEAGUES
8000 LEAGUES
9000 LEAGUES
10000 LEAGUES
11000 LEAGUES
12000 LEAGUES
13000 LEAGUES
14000 LEAGUES
15000 LEAGUES
16000 LEAGUES
17000 LEAGUES
18000 LEAGUES
19000 LEAGUES
20000 LEAGUES

sinking ...

sinking ...

SINK -O- METER®

1000 LEAGUES
2000 LEAGUES
3000 LEAGUES
4000 LEAGUES
5000 LEAGUES
6000 LEAGUES
7000 LEAGUES
8000 LEAGUES
9000 LEAGUES
10000 LEAGUES
11000 LEAGUES
12000 LEAGUES
13000 LEAGUES
14000 LEAGUES
15000 LEAGUES
16000 LEAGUES
17000 LEAGUES
18000 LEAGUES
19000 LEAGUES
20000 LEAGUES

96

97

and we write ...

You type so fast!

and we write …

and we write …

and we draw ...

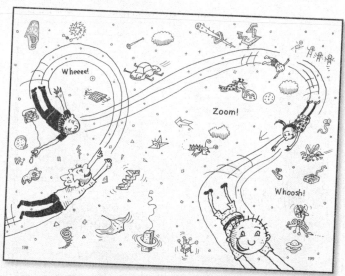

and we draw ...

I go to my shelf of learn to read books. I have one for each animal, including Andy and Terry.

'Who would like to read this one to them?' I say.
'I will,' says Albert.
He opens the book and starts reading.

A is for Andy. He writes the words.

B is for Barky. He barks at birds.

BARK!

C is for clones. They helped build the ramp.

D is for drawing. Terry's the champ!

and we draw …

Barely a moment elapses before Terence reappears, bearing aloft an enormous mallet.
'Hold still, Andy,' he says. 'This won't hurt a bit. Well, when I say it won't hurt a bit I mean, obviously, it will hurt a *lot*, so here goes …'

DONK!

'Is he all right?' says Alice.
'I'll check,' says Terence. He shakes my shoulder. 'Say something, Andy!'

'Um … er … ah … the sum of the square roots of any two sides of an isosceles triangle is equal to the square root of the remaining side.'

and we draw …

and we write …

and we write …

and, finally, we're done!

'Look!' says Albert, as we all pore over the pages. 'There's me!'

'And there's *me*!' says Alice.

'And there's *me*!' says Terry. 'Look, Andy! I'm in a book! I'm in a *book*!'

'You're in *every* book we write,' I remind him.

'So?' he says, shrugging. 'That doesn't make it any *less* exciting. Jill! I'm in a book ... and so is Andy ... and so are *you*!'

'Yes,' says Jill, 'and it's come out pretty good, too! In fact, I think it might be my favourite one yet.'

'Mine too!' says Terry. 'The only thing that could possibly make it even better is if we could push the big red button now. Can we, Andy? Can we push it?'

'Yes!' says Albert. 'Can we? Can we?'

'No!' I say. 'It's *too* dangerous! You heard what Madam Know-it-all said when we asked her about it. She saw a big explosion and then a whole bunch of DOOM!'

'But what if the big red thing Madam Know-it-all saw exploding *wasn't* the big red button?' says Terry. 'What if it was Mr Big Nose's big red nose exploding after she *pushed* him to the limit of his patience?'

'Yes!' says Jill. 'She did say herself that she didn't know absolutely everything, so it's possible she *may* have been wrong about the big red button.'

'I suppose it's *possible*,' I say, 'but I don't know—even if there's only a small chance that pushing the button will blow up the whole world, well, that's a pretty big risk to take …'

'But *not* pushing it is a pretty big risk to take too,' says Terry. 'We might miss out on something *really* amazing—like rainbows coming out of our noses, for instance.'

Brain-thinking noise

'*I* want a rainbow to come out of *my* nose,' says Albert.

'So do I!' says Alice, jumping up and down.

'It does sound quite nice,' says Jill. 'But, then, I wouldn't want the whole world to blow up.'

'All right,' I say. 'We'll take a vote. All in favour of pushing the big red button so we can find out what happens when we push the big red button, raise your hand!'

Terry and Alice and Albert put their hands in the air.

'Okay,' I say, 'now all those *not* in favour of pushing the big red button so we can find out what happens when we push the big red button, raise your hand!'

Me and Jill and Albert put our hands in the air. (Albert obviously doesn't understand what voting is—or maybe he just likes putting his hands in the air. But a vote *is* a vote, so I count it.)

'Three in favour and three not in favour,' I say.
  'It's a tie,' says Jill.

'What about the baby?' says Terry. 'The baby didn't vote.'

'Good point, Terry,' I say. 'But where *is* the baby?'

We look around.

OH NO! The baby is climbing up onto the big red button!

'No!' I yell.

But the baby just says, 'Goo-goo ga-ga!' and pulls itself up onto the button …

crawls towards the middle …

and plops down.

KA-CHUNK goes
the button.

'We're doomed!' I yell. 'We're all doomed! The baby has just pressed the big red button!'

'What do we do now?' says Terry.

'There's nothing we *can* do,' I say, 'except wait for our doom.'

'But *when* is it going to happen?' says Terry.

'Yeah, why is it taking so long?' says Albert.

'Yeah!' says Alice. 'You said the world was going to blow up! You promised!'

'I didn't *promise*,' I say. 'I said it *might* happen. Just be patient—you can't rush the end of the world. It will happen when it happens.'

'*If* it happens!' says Jill. 'I think it's looking more and more likely that Terry is right—Madam Know-it-all confused the big red button with Mr Big Nose's nose.'

'Bad luck, Andy,' says Terry. 'Sorry you were wrong about the world blowing up.'

'That's all right,' I say. 'Look on the bright side: the whole world didn't blow up.'

'Yeah, but look on the not-so-bright side,' says Terry. 'Rainbows didn't come out of our noses either.'

'Actually,' says Jill, 'speaking of noses, mine *does* feel kind of funny.'

'Is it tingling?' says Alice.

'Yes!' says Jill.

'Mine too!' says Alice.

'And mine,' says Albert.

'And mine!' says Terry. 'What about yours, Andy?'

'Well, I must admit, I do have a very odd sensation in my nose, but that doesn't mean ...'

Red

343

344

'We've got rainbows coming out of our noses, Andy!' says Terry. 'This is the best thing ever! And to think you didn't want to push the button!'

'It is very cool to have rainbows coming out of our noses, that's for sure,' I say. 'But what would make it the *best thing ever* would be if it could somehow help us to get our book—and the children—to Mr Big Nose on time.'

'Wow!' says Jill. 'Look at the size of the rainbow coming out of the Trunkinator's trunk! It's enormous!'

'Yeah,' says Terry. 'It goes all the way over the forest and into Mr Big Nose's office!'

'This is just what we need! We can use the rainbow as a bridge!' I say. 'Come on, everybody, jump on!'

We all climb up onto the Trunkinator's head and slide up the rainbow ...

Hee-haw!

and down into Mr Big Nose's office.

'Looks like our work here is done,' I say, as Alice, Albert and the baby hug Mr and Mrs Big Nose.

'I guess we'd better get back to the treehouse,' says Terry. 'Before the Trunkinator's trunk-rainbow fades.'

We are just about to climb back onto the rainbow when Alice and Albert come running over.

'Goodbye Andy, Terry and Jill,' says Albert. 'Thanks for the best babysitting day *ever*!'

'Goo-goo ga-ga,' says the baby.

'You're welcome,' I say. 'Come back whenever you like!'

'It was really nice to meet you,' says Jill. 'And thanks for all your help looking after Andy and Terry.'

'See you next time,' says Terry.

We turn to leave.

'Wait a minute,' says Alice. She takes a black texta and writes WORLD'S GREATEST BABYSITTERS on one of Mr Big Nose's publishing trophies.

'It's for all three of you,' says Alice.

'Thanks!' says Terry. 'We love it!'

'Yes!' I say. 'That's definitely going in the trophy room!'

We climb back
onto the rainbow
and slide up …

and back down into the treehouse.

'What are we going to do now?' says Terry.

'Build another 13 levels on our treehouse, of course,' I say.

'I *hoped* you were going to say that,' says Terry.

'I *knew* you were going to say that,' says Jill.

THE END

ANDY GRIFFITHS

The 130-STOREY TREEHOUSE

ILLUSTRATED BY

TERRY DENTON

COMING
20th OCTOBER
2020

The 13-Storey Treehouse

Andy and Terry's 13-storey treehouse is the most amazing treehouse in the world! It's got a bowling alley, a see-through swimming pool, a tank full of man-eating sharks, a giant catapult, a secret underground laboratory and a marshmallow machine that follows you around and shoots marshmallows into your mouth whenever you're hungry.

Well, what are you waiting for? Come on up!

The 26-Storey Treehouse

Join Andy and Terry in their newly expanded treehouse, which now features 13 brand-new storeys, including a dodgem car rink, a skate ramp, a mud-fighting arena, an anti-gravity chamber, an ice-cream parlour with 78 flavours run by an ice-cream serving robot called Edward Scooperhands and the Maze of Doom—a maze so complicated that nobody who has gone in has ever come out again … well, not yet, anyway.

Well, what are you waiting for? Come on up!

The 39-Storey Treehouse

Join Andy and Terry in their astonishing 39-storey treehouse! Jump on the world's highest trampoline, toast marshmallows in an active volcano, swim in the chocolate waterfall, pat baby dinosaurs, go head-to-trunk with The Trunkinator, break out your best moves on the dance floor, fly in a jet-propelled swivel chair, ride a terrifying rollercoaster and meet Professor Stupido, the world's greatest UN-inventor.

Well, what are you waiting for? Come on up!

The 52-Storey Treehouse

Andy and Terry's incredible, ever-expanding treehouse has 13 new storeys, including a watermelon-smashing level, a wave machine, a life-size snakes and ladders game (with real ladders and real snakes!), a rocket-powered carrot-launcher, a Ninja Snail Training Academy and a high-tech detective agency with all the latest high-tech detective technology, which is lucky because they have a BIG mystery to solve—*where is Mr Big Nose???*

Well, what are you waiting for? Come on up!

The 65-Storey Treehouse

Andy and Terry's amazing 65-storey treehouse now has a pet-grooming salon, a birthday room where it's always your birthday (even when it's not), a room full of exploding eyeballs, a lollipop shop, a quicksand pit, an ant farm, a time machine and Tree-NN: a 24-hour-a-day TV news centre keeping you up to date with all the latest treehouse news, current events and gossip.

Well, what are you waiting for? Come on up!

The 78-Storey Treehouse

Join Andy and Terry in their spectacular new 78-storey treehouse. They've added 13 new levels including a drive-thru car wash, a combining machine, a scribbletorium, an ALL-BALL sports stadium, Andyland, Terrytown, a high-security potato chip storage facility and an open-air movie theatre.

Well, what are you waiting for? Come on up!

The 91-Storey Treehouse

Join Andy and Terry in their latest mind-blowing ever-growing treehouse. Go for a spin in the world's most powerful whirlpool, take a ride in a submarine sandwich, get marooned on a desert island, hang out in a giant spider web, visit the fortune teller's tent to get your fortune told by Madam Know-it-all and decide whether or not to push the mysterious big red button ...

Well, what are you waiting for? Come on up!

The 104-Storey Treehouse

Join Andy and Terry in their wonderfully wild and wacky 104-storey treehouse. You can throw some refrigerators, make money with the money-making machine (or honey if you'd prefer—it makes that too), climb the never-ending staircase, have a bunfight, deposit some burps in the burp bank, get totally tangled up in the tangled-up level, or just take some time out and relax in the beautiful sunny meadow full of buttercups, butterflies and bluebirds.

Well, what are you waiting for? Come on up!

The 117-Storey Treehouse

Andy and Terry's amazing treehouse now has 13 new storeys, including a tiny-horse level, a pyjama-party room, an Underpants Museum, a photo-bombing booth, a waiting room, a Door of Doom, a circus, a giant-robot-fighting arena, a traffic school, a water-ski park filled with flesh-eating piranhas and a treehouse visitor centre with a 24-hour information desk, a penguin-powered flying treehouse tour bus and a gift shop.

Well, what are you waiting for? Come on up!

The Treehouse Fun Books

Andy, Terry and Jill love having fun in the treehouse.
And now it's your turn! There's stuff to write, pictures to draw,
puzzles to solve and SO MUCH MORE!

So, what are you waiting for? Come on up!